THE LEGEND OF DAVE THE VILLAGER 1

by Dave Villager

Third Print Edition (August 2019)

BOOK ONE:
The Adventure Begins

CHAPTER ONE

The Secret Stronghold

BAM BAM BAM!

Dave awoke with a start. Someone was punching a hole in his bedroom wall.

He rubbed the sleep from his eyes and saw that most of his room was gone. His parents smiled back at him from what was left of the lounge. The morning light shone down from holes in the roof.

"What happened to the house?" he asked.

"Steve has blessed us!" said his mom happily. "He's using blocks from our house to build one of his masterpieces!"

A fist punched through his wall—BAM BAM BAM!

The wall disappeared to reveal a man in a light blue t-shirt and jeans.

"It's Steve!" said Dave's dad, clambering over the remains of the kitchen to get into Dave's bedroom. He ran up to the blue-t-shirted figure and knelt down before him.

"Thank you Steve, for blessing our home, thank you, thank you."

Dave's mom came over and knelt next to her husband.

"It's an honor Steve," she said. "Thank you so much."

Dave got out of bed, frowning.

"Steve, you've destroyed our house!"

"Have I destroyed it, bro?" said Steve, grinning at him, "Or have I *improved* it!"

"No," said Dave, "you've definitely destroyed it."

"Just come and see!" said Steve, and ran off. Dave and his parents followed him outside.

The village was a mess. All the houses had bits missing, and there were huge holes in the ground too. The villagers were all gathered outside, looking on in awe as Steve finished building a huge structure where the town hall used to be.

"It's so beautiful, Steve!" said one villager.

"Great work, Steve!" said another.

Dave looked up at the structure as Steve put the finishing touches to it. At first he couldn't work out what it was supposed to be, but then he realized—it was a huge wooden statue... of Steve.

"You destroyed our village to make a statue of yourself?!" Dave said, angrily. Steve jumped down from the top of the statue's head and landed in front of him.

"Cool, isn't it?"

Before Dave could speak, the other villagers all flocked round Steve, shaking his hand and congratulating him.

"Amazing work, Steve!"

"Another masterpiece!"

Dave sighed. It was always the same. Dave was a villager—and villagers were all meant to love Steve.

Steve went on adventures, killed monsters and built huge, pointless things, but villagers did none of that.

"Remember Dave," his mother told him once, when he was still a baby villager, "a villager has two purposes in life: to stand around all day doing nothing, and to trade emeralds with Steve."

"What about Grandma?" he asked. "She's a witch. Can't I be a witch?"

"We don't talk about Grandma," she said.

But Dave had never bought into all that. Why couldn't he go on an adventure? Why couldn't he kill monsters and build things?

Steve pushed away from the crowd of admiring villagers.

"Thank you, you're all too kind."

He walked over to a switch stuck to the side of the statue's leg.

"And now, for the grand finale, I'm going to blow the

statue up!"

Everyone clapped and cheered.

"Wait, what?" said Dave.

Steve put a hand on Dave's shoulder.

"I've filled the statue with TNT blocks, and now I'm going to blow it up! How awesome is that going to be!"

"But Steve... the statue's in the middle of our village."

"I know," grinned Steve, "how lucky are you—you all get front row seats for the explosion!"

Dave turned to the other villagers.

"You're ok with him destroying our village?"

"It will be an honor to have our village destroyed by a great hero like Steve," said the Mayor, sticking his chest out proudly.

"But we're all going to be blown to bits," said Dave.

"It will be an honor to be blown to bits by a great hero like Steve," said the Mayor.

Dave rolled his eyes.

"You're all crazy," he said.

"Don't worry," said Steve, "I'm going to give you all plenty of warning—no-one's going to get hurt." He flipped the switch. "Ok, everyone run!"

Steve ran off as fast as his legs could carry him. With terrified yelling and screaming, the villagers ran off after him.

KABOOM!!!

Thankfully everyone made it out in time, but Dave was horrified to see his village—the place he'd lived his entire life—in ruins. All that was left was a blocky, gray pit.

The villagers—seemingly forgetting that a moment ago they'd been running for their lives—all cheered.

"Top job, Steve old chap!" said the Mayor. "That was an amazing explosion!"

"Thanks bro," said Steve, "but you guys are the real heroes. Actually, who am I kidding—I'm the real hero. Obviously."

"Look," someone shouted from the edge of the pit, "there's something down there!"

The explosion had revealed some sort of ancient underground building. There were stone brick walls and pits of lava.

Old Man Johnson, the oldest villager, waddled over with his walking stick.

"Well, I'll be—it's a stronghold! I remember hearing legends about these when I was a boy. I never dreamed there was one underneath our village all this time!"

"That's why you wanted to blow up our village, Steve, isn't that right?" said Dave's mum. "You knew there was a stronghold underneath!"

"Er, yeah," said Steve, "that was why. It definitely wasn't just because I thought it would be funny."

They all made their way carefully down the crater where the village used be. Steve built some wooden steps so they could all go through the hole in the ceiling and down into the stronghold.

Over a pit of lava there was a square frame made up of single blocks, half of which were gone. Most of the blocks had weird green things in them that looked like eyes.

"It's an end portal," said Old Man Johnson, "the Ancients built them long ago to travel to the End."

"What's the End?" asked Dave.

"I've heard of the End!" said Steve. "It's where the ender dragon lives! Get that portal fired up, old timer—I've got a dragon to slay!"

"I'm afraid I can't," said Old Man Johnson. "It seems that some of the blocks of the frame were destroyed in the explosion. The portal is broken."

Steve was disappointed, but soon took his mind off it by checking the stronghold for treasure.

Dave had a look round too, and found a small underground library. Most of the books had been destroyed by old age or by the explosion, but one caught his eye. The title on the cover was *How to get to the End*.

Most of the pages crumbled to dust when he tried to read them, but there was one passage that had an image that looked familiar: a picture of a scary-looking green eye. Underneath the picture was a caption: *An eye of ender*.

Dave read the passage. The language was old and difficult to understand, but after a few reads he realized what it was telling him to do.

Most of the villagers were still gathered in the portal room as Dave returned, the book under his arm.

"I guess we should find somewhere to build ourselves a new village," Dave overheard one of them say.

"Maybe we could build it in a mushroom biome," another villager replied, "I always fancied myself as a mooshroom farmer."

Dave walked up the stone steps that led to the end portal.

"Dave, what are you doing?" his mother said, running up to him. "Be careful of the lava!"

"Don't worry Mum," Dave replied, "I know what I'm doing."

There were only seven of the end portal frame blocks left. Dave could see from the design that there were meant to be twelve—five had been destroyed or lost.

Six of the remaining seven had *ender eyes* inside them —the strange eye objects that Dave had seen the picture of in the book.

He reached down and pulled one of the ender eyes out. It was a round disk with a thin black pupil in the middle. If Dave hadn't known better, he would have sworn the eye was looking at him—it was creepy.

Dave carefully made his way around the lava pit, removing the other ender eyes until he had all six. Then he walked up the wooden stairs to the edge of the crater that had been his village. After being underground so long, his eyes stung from the bright sunlight. The other villagers followed behind him, curious about what he was going to do.

Dave climbed to the top of the crater and stood on the grass. The other villagers stood around him.

"What's going on, bro?" said Steve. "Hey, those little eye things are cool. Can I have one? I'll give you one emerald for the lot."

These are ender eyes," Dave said. "If what I read is correct, they should reveal the location of the nearest working end portal. And this time, I'm going to be the one who finds it—I'll find the end portal, slay the ender dragon, and be a hero!"

"Er, villagers can't be heroes, bro," said Steve. "Only Steves can be heroes. And I'm the only Steve."

"Well, maybe villagers can be heroes too," said Dave, "it's just that they've never tried before."

Dave threw an ender eye into the air. It hovered there for a moment, then zoomed off towards the horizon.

"It worked!" said Dave, laughing, "It actually worked! It went north, so all I have to do is head north and I'll eventually get to another stronghold!"

Suddenly, Steve grabbed the other five ender eyes out of Dave's hands.

"Hey!" said Dave. "Give those back!"

"I'm sorry, little buddy," Steve replied, "but as a hero it would be irresponsible for me to let you go off and search for dragons. I know my life must seem really cool, but it's too dangerous for someone like you. You're a villager—you should be doing villager things. Like, I dunno, growing wheat?"

Steve whistled and a horse came running over. He jumped on its back.

"Sorry fans, I've got to split. I've got a dragon to kill!"

And with that, he rode off.

"That's not fair!" said Dave. "Those were my ender eyes!"

Dave's mum and dad came over. Dave's dad put a hand on his shoulder.

"It's for the best son," he said. "Adventuring is for Steves, not villagers."

The villagers started to walk away. Eventually Dave was standing all by himself. Sadly, he took another look at the book.

Old Man Johnson came hobbling over.

"Don't listen to them, Dave. When I was your age I wanted to go on adventures too—and everyone always told me not to go. I wish I'd never listened to them. It's too late for me, but perhaps not for you."

He handed Dave an old book.

"*A beginners guide to crafting,*" Dave said, reading the cover.

"Now you can craft, just like Steve!"

"This is amazing, thank you!" Dave said, flicking through the pages. Then he saw something that made his heart leap.

"They have how to make ender eyes in here!" said Dave happily. "Wait, what's blaze powder?"

"The recipe for that is in there too," said Old Man Johnson. "That book won't have every crafting recipe ever, but it should get you started at least."

"I don't know what to say."

"Just promise me you'll defeat the ender dragon before Steve does, and prove once and for all that villagers can be heroes."

"I promise!"

Dave's parents weren't happy when he told them he was going on an adventure, but in the end they had to accept it.

"Just be careful," his mum told him as they said their goodbyes. "Watch out for creepers and if you see an enderman, stare at it to keep it away. Or was that *don't* stare at it? I never can remember..."

"Goodbye, Dave," said his dad. "I got you this—I hope it helps."

He handed Dave an iron sword.

"The blacksmith made it. He says he normally only makes them for Steve, but he made an exception."

"Thanks, Dad."

And after a big hug with both his parents, Dave was off on his adventure.

CHAPTER TWO

Dave on the Road

The sun was shining and the birds were singing as Dave set out. He'd never been very far from the village before, and was enjoying the walk. The hills around him were green and blocky, and cows and sheep watched him as he walked past.

By midday he was feeling hungry, so he found a pig and hit it with his sword until it turned into porkchops.

He tried to eat the chops raw, but the taste was horrible. Back home his father had done all of the cooking, so Dave turned to the book the old man had given him for advice.

"How to build a furnace..." he said, starting to read. "Eight cobblestone blocks needed. Where do I get cobblestone from?"

Crafting, it seemed, was more complicated than Dave had thought it would be. To get cobblestone, you needed to dig up stone. To dig up stone you needed a pickaxe. To craft a pickaxe you needed a crafting table. To make a crafting table you needed wood. It made Dave's brain hurt.

So it all started with wood. Dave went up to a tree. There were hundreds of them about, all made of wood. But how was he supposed to get the wood from them? He'd seen a crafting recipe for an axe in the book, but to make an axe you needed wood.

He tapped the tree lightly with his hand. The smallest of cracks appeared in the grain for a split second, but then it was gone. He tapped it again and the crack reappeared; then again, and more cracks appeared. He started to punch it, the cracks spreading across the wood. Finally the tree block broke, leaving a gap in the middle of the tree's trunk.

On the ground was a tiny block—a miniature version of the wood block that had been part of the tree's trunk. Dave picked it up, looking at it in amazement. He wanted to take another look at his book, to remind him of how to craft a pickaxe, but when he placed the wood block on the floor, something amazing happened—it turned back into a full-sized wooden block.

He tried to pick it up again, but the block was stuck to the floor. He punched it and it broke again—turning back into a miniature block.

"Weird," he thought. He placed the tiny block in his backpack. Thankfully it didn't turn back into a full-sized block this time.

He knew he might need quite a lot of wood for building, so he went back to the tree, breaking the remaining blocks until the tree's trunk was no more, and the leaves above faded into nothing.

Following the instructions in the book, he placed one of the tiny wood blocks in the palm of his hand and waited. He didn't have to wait long: in less than a couple of seconds there was a *POP*, and the wooden block had turned into four tiny blocks of wooden planks.

He made a few plank blocks, then put four of them together in his hand, where they merged into a tiny crafting table.

He slammed the crafting table into the ground and, as if by magic, it grew into a full-sized crafting table.

"That is so cool," said Dave, grinning to himself. The table had a nine-square grid carved onto its surface. Each of the nine squares was the same size as the tiny blocks.

Dave took another look at his book. To make a wooden pickaxe he needed wooden planks and sticks. He had the planks, but no sticks—so he looked up the recipe. He placed two tiny wooden plank blocks on the crafting table, and they transformed into a bunch of sticks.

Next he placed three wooden plank blocks along the top three squares of the crafting table, and two sticks underneath. There was a *POP* and suddenly a pickaxe appeared. His very first tool.

"Awesome!" said Dave. He immediately started to dig at the soil, but his pickaxe barely did any damage to it. With a *SNAP* the pickaxe broke.

Dave went back to the book and saw that for mud and sand a shovel worked better. So he made one, as well as a new wooden pickaxe.

The book also explained how you could use tools to dig up materials to make better tools. A wooden pickaxe could dig up cobblestone to make a stone pickaxe, a stone pickaxe could dig up iron to make an iron pickaxe (with a bit of help from some smelting to turn the iron ore into ingots) and so on. The best tools, according to the book, were made of diamond, but diamond was very rare.

"One day I'll have all diamond tools and weapons," Dave thought, looking through the book. The book said you could even make armor for horses out of diamond. "I'd be invincible," Dave said to himself, "wearing diamond armor and riding a diamond-armored horse!"

On the page about tools there was a message written in the margin in red ink—it looked like the old man had written it on the page himself.

NEVER DIG STRAIGHT DOWN!

Dave took his shovel and started to dig. Following the old man's advice he dug down in a diagonal direction. He dug through a few dirt blocks, then reached stone—so he changed to his pickaxe.

It was slow going. Every stone block he broke turned into cobblestone. Just like the wood, the cobblestone blocks were tiny, and he was able to fit them in his backpack.

Eventually he realized that he wouldn't be able to go any further without torches.

He made his way back up the stone corridor he'd dug, making his way back up towards the light. His rucksack was full of cobblestone, making the going slow.

When he got back outside the sun was beginning to set. He looked in his rucksack and was pleased to see that he had found some coal. It had been so dark in the tunnel that he'd thought it had all been cobblestone.

He used the crafting table to make a furnace: eight cobblestone blocks with a gap in the middle. Then he placed the furnace next to the crafting table.

The book said that wood or coal (or quite a few other things) could be used as fuel for the furnace, but Dave decided to use wood, as he wanted to save the coal for making torches (a piece of coal on top of a stick, according to the book).

He lit the furnace and sat in front of it, enjoying the warmth as his porkchop cooked.

When it was done he gobbled it up in seconds, he was so hungry. Then he started cooking a second.

After eating his third porkchop he sat down and enjoyed the cool evening air. The sun had almost set now, and it was getting properly dark.

"Maybe I could sleep out in the open tonight," he thought. The weather was warm and the idea of looking up at the stars all night appealed to him.

Then he heard a noise that chilled his soul.

"BURRRRRR!!!"

Something was walking towards him through the darkness. He quickly crafted a torch and placed it down in front of him.

"Er, hello?" Dave said. "Who's there?"

A figure stepped into the torchlight. For a moment Dave thought it was Steve, but then he saw its rotted green skin and black eyes—it was a zombie!

Another zombie appeared out of the darkness, then another, until a whole crowd of them were surrounding Dave

"Get back!" he yelled, shaking his sword at them.

He was surrounded, with no way out. There were zombies on every side.

"What am I going to do?" he thought. Was this how it was going to end for him—eaten by zombies on the very first night of his big adventure?

A zombie started to waddle closer. Dave swung his sword, hitting the zombie on the head. The zombie groaned and stepped backwards. Dave swung his sword again, as a warning, but his pickaxe fell off his belt, clattering on the grass.

And that gave Dave an idea.

NEVER DIG STRAIGHT DOWN the old man's note in the book had warned. But down was the only safe way for Dave to go. He grabbed his pickaxe and started to dig.

His pickaxe cut through block after block, and the small square of night sky above got smaller and smaller. The zombies were looking down at him, groaning with frustration at having missed out on their dinner.

"I'll just go a bit further down," he thought, "then I'll wait until daylight and dig my way to the surface again."

Then he cut through a block and suddenly there was nothing below his feet.

"So that's why you don't dig straight down," he thought, as he fell through the roof of a cavern towards a huge lake of lava.

CHAPTER THREE

Porkins

"Waaaaaaaa!!!"

Dave fell towards the lava, flailing his arms like a crazy person.

He closed his eyes, then landed on something hard.

"Is this heaven?" he wondered.

He opened his eyes and saw that he wasn't in heaven: he was lying on a tiny block of stone, which lay in the middle of the lava lake.

For a moment he was overjoyed at being alive—then he realized that he was trapped. There was lava on every side, and no way out.

What was he going to do? He tried to think what Steve would do. Steve liked to build things, kill things and blow things up. He had no TNT, so blowing stuff up was out of the question, there was nothing to kill... so maybe he could build his way out?

Suddenly his little stone platform lit up. He looked up

and saw light shining down from the tiny square hole far above him. It was day time again.

"I can build my way up!" Dave yelled happily. He pulled out a tiny cobblestone block from his backpack, jumped up and placed it below his feet—where it turned into a full-sized block. He did this again and again, until he was standing on a tall tower, far above the lava.

He reached into his backpack to grab some more cobblestone, but accidentally dropped the bag—its contents spilling out and falling into the lava below!

Thankfully Dave managed to keep hold of the bag, and his two books didn't fall out, but most of his blocks were gone. He had nowhere near enough to build his way up to the surface.

He was in a worse predicament than before now—stuck on a tower in the middle of a lake of lava.

"Help!" Dave yelled desperately. "Someone help me!"

He sighed and sat down. He was all alone, there was no-one here to save him. He should have listened to his parents and Steve—villagers weren't meant to go on adventures. This had all been a big mistake.

"Ahoy there!"

Dave jumped so much he nearly fell off of his tower. He looked around to try and see where the voice had come from.

"I say, down here!"

Dave looked down and saw a pig standing by the edge of the lava lake. Wait, he thought, pigs can't stand... but this one was definitely standing; standing on two legs.

"Hello there!" said the standing pig.

"Er, hello," said Dave.

"Need a hand?" asked the pig.

"Yes please."

The pig started throwing blocks of sand into the lava. The sand soaked up the lava and sunk to the bottom of it. Soon the pig had built a sand bridge all the way across the lava lake to Dave's tower.

Dave dug his way down, destroying each block of his tower until he was just above the lake. Then he jumped down onto the pig's sand bridge.

"This way," said the pig, leading Dave across the bridge to the side of the lake. When he got back to solid ground, Dave breathed a big sigh of relief.

"Thank you!" he said to the pig. "I thought my bacon was cooked! Uh, no offense."

"Happy to help!" said the pig. "My name is Porkins."

"Dave," said Dave.

"Well met, Dave," said the pig.

"I don't want to be rude," said Dave, "but I've never met a pig who can talk before."

"That because I'm not a pig," said the pig, "I'm a

24

pigman."

"Ah, ok," said Dave. He decided not to point out that he'd never heard of a pigman before either.

"Would you like something to eat?" Porkins asked.

"Yes please," said Dave, "I'd love some baco—I mean, anything. Any food would be great."

Porkins led him down some torch-lit tunnels until they reached a steel door, set into a flat, gray stone wall. A sign next to the door said: *Porkins's House.*

Porkins pulled a switch next to the door and it swung open. Dave followed him inside.

Porkins's home was surprisingly cosy, with lots of pictures on the stone walls and wooden furniture. Dave sat down as the pigman cooked some mushroom stew in the furnace.

When the stew was ready, the two of them ate at the wooden table. After Dave finished, Porkins made him some pumpkin pie. When the meal was finally over, Dave was stuffed.

"Phew," said Dave. "I ate like a pig! Uh, no offense."

But Porkins didn't seem to take offense at anything. He was always happy and smiling.

"How come you live underground?" Dave asked him. "Or is that something all pigmen do?"

A dark look crossed Porkins's face.

"I'm the only pigman left, I'm afraid," said Porkins

sadly. "I moved underground as it reminds me of my home."

Dave wanted to ask Porkins what had happened to the other pigmen, but Porkins looked so sad that he decided now wasn't the time.

"I'm from a village," Dave said, "on the surface. I'm on a quest to hunt down the ender dragon."

"Why?" Porkins asked. "Did it do something bad?"

"Well, no," said Dave, "but it's a dragon, and it's a hero's job to slay dragons."

"Fair enough," said Porkins. "Can I come with you?"

Dave was taken aback.

"It's going to be very dangerous," he told the pigman. "I mean I'll probably have to fight all sorts of monsters on the way. And then there's the dragon."

"That's fine," said Porkins, "it all sounds spiffing, actually. I've been bored out of my mind living by myself. An adventure sounds just the ticket!"

"I mean, you'll need a sword," said Dave. "And as I said, it will be very dangerous."

Dave had always thought of adventures as something you did on your own: a hero out in the wild with just his sword to protect him. As nice as Porkins seemed to be, Dave thought he'd just get in the way.

"Will this do?" Porkins asked. He opened a chest and

pulled out a sword with a shimmering blue blade.

Dave's mouth dropped open.

"Is that... is that..." he mumbled, unable to get his words out.

"Diamond!" said Porkins, happily. "There's not much to do down here except mine. I've got a spare if you'd like it."

He pulled out a second diamond sword and handed it to Dave.

"T-thank you!" said Dave.

"No problem," smiled Porkins. "I'm sure you'd do the same for me, as a friend."

Dave grinned. Maybe having a companion on his quest wouldn't be so bad after all.

That night they stayed at Porkins's house. Dave slept on the spare bed ("no-one's ever used it before!" Porkins happily informed him), then in the morning Porkins made them breakfast (Dave stopped himself from asking for bacon, just in time).

Porkins packed a rucksack (Dave noticed there were a lot of diamonds, coal and other blocks in there) and then they set off on their journey.

CHAPTER FOUR

Carl

"I think this way leads back to the surface," said Porkins. "Although it's been a while, so I might be wrong."

They were making their way through a vast underground cave system. Porkins had plenty of coal and Dave had a few bits of wood left in his bag that hadn't fallen into the lava, so they made some torches and placed them down as they went along.

"Are there monsters in these caves?" Dave asked.

"Oh yes, lots!" said Porkins happily.

Suddenly a pack of flying creatures burst out from the darkness, flapping past Dave.

"Monsters!" he yelled. "Help me!"

The creatures flew off, back into the darkness.

Porkins laughed.

"Don't worry, those were just bats. They're harmless."

"Harmless. Right," said Dave, feeling his cheeks glow red. "I knew that."

Then they heard a sound coming from the darkness:
"BUUUUURR!"

"Zombies!" said Dave. "I'd know that sound anywhere."

He and Porkins pulled out their diamond swords.

Suddenly zombies came out of the darkness, surrounding them on all sides. Dave's hands were sweaty and he was nervous, but then he remembered that he had a diamond sword. A diamond sword!

"Rrraghhh!" he yelled, running at the zombies. He hit one in the head with his diamond blade and it was immediately destroyed. One hit was all it took for each zombie, and he and Porkins cut through them like butter.

Finally the zombies were all slain, leaving just piles of rotten flesh behind—which Dave stuffed into his backpack. He didn't know if you could craft anything with it, but he thought it might come in useful later.

"That was fun!" said Porkins.

"Yeah," said Dave, grinning. "It was, actually."

Then he heard a sound that chilled him to the bone:
"HIIIISSSSS!!!"

"Creeper!" Dave yelled. A green creature with black eyes and a gaping mouth emerged from the shadows.

Dave pushed Porkins out of the way, and the two of them fell off a cliff edge as the creeper exploded behind them.

For the second time in two days, Dave found himself falling—but this time he landed in water. He and Porkins were washed away by an underground river, Dave trying desperately to grab onto the sides and get out, but the water was moving too fast.

Dave wasn't very good at swimming, and tried desperately to keep his head above water as the current swept them down into the darkness of the caves.

Suddenly the river ended, and he found himself falling again—and landed in lake. He splashed around, trying to find the shore, but the lake seemed to be huge. In the dark he could hear a waterfall, where the river flowed through the ceiling into the lake.

He kept swimming, terrified of what kind of creatures could be below him in the dark water, until he reached the shore, and clambered out.

"Porkins?" he yelled. There was no answer. He was all alone.

Dave reached into his bag for a torch, but his bag was gone. A cold trickle of fear ran down his spine. He was deep underground, in the dark, with no torches and no tools. What was he going to do?

Then, just as he thought things couldn't get any worse, he heard the sound he feared the most:

"HISSSSSSSS!"

He was too shocked to run, so just stupidly covered his face with his hands. But after a few seconds there was no explosion.

Then the noise came again, it sounded like it was right next to him:

"HISSSSSSSSSS!"

But still no explosion.

"Oh come on," said a voice nearby. "why isn't this working?"

Another voice came out of the darkness, this one further away: "Come on, blow him up!"

"I'm trying," said the first voice. "HISS! HISS! HISSSSS! I'm not exploding."

There was laughter—three or four voices, it sounded like.

"What kind of creeper can't even explode?" said a third voice.

"Shut up!" said the first voice. "I'll do it, ok? I just need some time."

"You've had your chance," said the third voice, "and you failed. Let me try. HISSSSSS!!!!"

Dave ran. He couldn't see where he was going, but he had to get away from the creepers.

"Now he's getting away!" one of them yelled. "Great job, Carl!"

Dave stumbled through the dark, feeling his way along the walls. He ran and ran until he was sure he must have lost them.

But they can see in the dark, he thought unhappily, *and I can't.*

What was he going to do? He could be wandering these caves forever and never find his way out, but he had to try.

He walked on for what seemed like hours, keeping his ears peeled for monsters and hoping desperately to come across some light.

He wondered what had happened to Porkins. Had he managed to get out of the river before it flowed into the lake? Or had something terrible happened to him?

Dave thought about trying to build some tools in the dark, but everything required wood. He tried punching stone, but it took forever to destroy it with just his fists, and without using a pickaxe it didn't drop any cobblestone, so he couldn't have made stone tools anyway.

No, his only hope was that he'd come across a passage that led back to the surface. But he was so deep now that it didn't seem very likely.

"Hello," said a voice.

Dave jumped.

"Who's there?!" He reached for his sword, but remembered he didn't have one.

"Don't worry," said the voice, "I'm not here to blow you up."

"You—you're a creeper?"

"Yeah. I'm the one who tried to blow you up by the lake. Sorry about that."

Dave was confused—and still quite terrified.

"So if you don't want to blow me up, what do you want?"

"My friends have kicked me out of their gang," said the creeper, sounding sad. "They say a creeper who can't explode is no creeper at all. So I thought I'd join you."

"Join me?"

"Yes. Look, I'll level with you. You look like a bit of an idiot, but I've lost all my friends and I've got no family—"

"What happened to your family?"

"They blew my themselves up. Obviously. That's what every creeper should do. But for some reason, I can't."

"Why would you want to blow yourself up anyway?" Dave asked.

"Because that's what creepers do!" said the creeper, annoyed. "Anyway, no creepers will let me in their gang now, and you're the only non-creeper I know, so I'm going to join you."

"Right," said Dave. He didn't know what was worse—a creeper who wanted to blow you up or one that wanted to be your friend. But then an idea struck him.

"Can you help me find my way to the surface?" he asked the creeper.

Probably not," said the creeper. "But I can try, I guess. Just follow me."

"I can't see you," said Dave. "I can't see in the dark."

"Right," said the creeper. "Just follow my voice then. I'm Carl, by the way."

"Dave," said Dave.

"That's a stupid name," said the creeper. "Trust me to get stuck with a Dave."

CHAPTER FIVE

Captured by Zombies!

"Keep going," said Carl, "follow my voice."

Dave had been following Carl the creeper for hours through the darkness. He kept thinking about Porkins, and hoped the pigman was ok. As annoying as he was, he'd been better than Carl the creeper: who was constantly moaning.

"The surface is overrated anyway," said Carl. "Dunno why you'd want to go up there in the first place."

"That's where I'm from," Dave told him. "I'm on a quest to kill a dragon."

"Sounds like a pretty stupid quest to me," said Carl.

Suddenly Carl stopped, and Dave walked straight into him.

"Shush," said Carl.

"What is it?" Dave asked.

"Zombies up ahead. I can hear them."

Dave could hear them too now, making their usual

"BUUUURR" sounds. It sounded like there were a lot of them. He could see the slight glow of torchlight too, up in the distance.

"We'll have to go the long way round," said Carl.

Then, amongst the zombie sounds, Dave heard something else:

"I say chaps, this is all very spiffing!"

His heart sank.

"They've got Porkins," he said.

"Who's Porkins?" asked Carl.

"He was traveling with me. He's a pigman."

"What's a pigman?"

"It's a bit like a pig, but a bit like a man as well."

"Well," said Carl, "whatever he is, he's going to be zombie food in a few minutes. We need to go the long way round, or we'll end up being the same."

"We can't leave him!" said Dave. "He's my... my sort-of friend."

Carl sighed.

"Well, you can go rescue your sort-of friend by yourself," he said. "I'm staying here. If you survive, come back and find me."

"I thought you were in my gang?" said Dave. "Gangs stick together, I always thought."

The creeper sighed again.

"Ok, ok, I'll help your stupid pig friend. Although by the time we get there he'll probably be roasted with an apple in his mouth."

"Then we'd better move quickly," said Dave.

He and Carl crept forward towards the torchlight. Dave could just about see now, and he got his first glimpse of Carl. Carl was a normal creeper, but about a head shorter than they usually were.

They finally reached the edge of a cliff, and below them a big group of zombies were gathered around a campfire. Tied up with rope, sitting against a wall, was Porkins. As ever, he was smiling.

"Is dat fire ready yet?" one of the zombies asked. "I'm starving."

"Me too," said Porkins. "What are we eating?"

"What an idiot," Carl whispered to Dave.

"Fire ready now," another zombie said. "Let's get cooking."

Four of the zombies waddled over and picked Porkins up. They tied him to a pole.

"Is this a prank, chaps?" Porkins asked. "This is terribly fun, but I'm afraid I must be off soon—I need to find my friend Dave. He's a villager, I don't suppose you've seen him?"

"If we see him, we eat him too," said a zombie.

"Eat him?" said Porkins, confused. "Why would you... oh dear."

His face fell, as he finally realized what was about to happen. The zombies carried him towards the fire.

"I must say, I doubt I'll taste very nice," said Porkins nervously. "Very tough meat, I suspect."

"Well, what now?" whispered Carl. "We don't have any swords."

Dave had been thinking the same thing. How were they going to save Porkins without ending up cooking on the fire as well? Then he looked at Carl and had an idea.

The zombies placed Porkins's pole above the fire, and started to turn it.

"I must say, this is a bit too hot for my liking," said Porkins. "If anyone can hear me—HELP!!"

"Get away from him!"

The zombies all turned round. Dave was holding Carl the creeper out in front of him.

"Get away from him, or I'll blow us all to smithereens!" said Dave.

"I hate to remind you," Carl whispered to him, "but I can't blow anyone to smithereens. I can't explode!"

"Yes," Dave whispered back, "but they don't know that."

He moved forward. The zombies started to back away.

"That's it," said Dave, "keep away."

"Dave!" said Porkins happily. "I knew you'd come for me! Everyone, this is my best friend Dave."

"Well, I don't know about best friend," said Dave, "we've only known each other a day..."

"Only a day, but I know he's going to be my BFF," Porkins told the zombies. "Now Dave old chap, would you mind getting me down from this spit? It's a bit hot. I think there's some sand in my bag."

Dave saw that Porkins's bag and—to his delight—his own, had been left in the corner of the room. He put Carl down and ran over to Porkins's bag, taking out a block of sand, then ran back and placed it on top of the fire, putting it out. He started to untie Porkins.

The zombies were still watching cautiously from the corners of the room.

"Get out of here," Dave told them, or my creeper will blow you all to bits!"

The zombies stayed where they were.

"I'll sort this out," said Carl. He slithered towards the zombies.

"HIIIISSS!"

At the sound of the hissing, the zombies all ran, pushing and shoving each other in a mad dash to escape. Within a few seconds there was no sign of them, leaving just Dave, Carl and Porkins in the torch-lit room.

Dave finished untying Porkins. Porkins let go of the pole and landed on his feet. He gave Dave a hug.

"Thank you Dave!" he said. "You really are a hero! That dragon doesn't stand a chance."

He turned to Carl.

"And thank you too, little man," Porkins said. "I don't think I've had the pleasure?"

"This is Carl," said Dave. "He's a creeper. A friendly one. Sort of."

"What do you mean, 'sort of'?" said Carl. "I'll have you know that for a creeper I'm amazingly friendly. I didn't blow you up, did I?"

"You did try to," said Dave.

"A friendly creeper," said Porkins, grinning, "what fun! I just know we're all going to be such good friends."

"I've never wanted to blow someone up more in my whole life," said Carl.

They had no idea where they were, but with the torches from Dave's bag and Carl being able to see in the dark, they headed off on their quest to find the surface.

It didn't take long before they saw rays of light up ahead.

"Daylight!" said Dave happily.

He ran on ahead, until he came out of a cave and

found himself on a mountain overlooking a lush green valley below. After being underground for so long, it was the most beautiful sight he'd ever seen.

Porkins and Carl came out behind him.

"Isn't it wonderful?" Dave said.

"No," said Carl. "Not really."

CHAPTER SIX

The Portal

After chopping some trees down for wood, they built themselves a little cabin by a lake—to protect them from monsters at night and give them somewhere to plan their next steps.

Dave looked through the book Old Man Johnson had given him. He had no idea where he was and had no ender eyes left, so he'd have to make some more if he was going to find his way to another stronghold.

He looked up the recipe for ender eyes. To make one you needed an ender pearl and some blaze powder.

"Where do you get ender pearls from?" Dave wondered. A shiver of terror went through him when he saw the answer: they were dropped by slain endermen.

Since he was little, Dave had been terrified of endermen. He'd never seen one in person, but he'd heard the legends. Endermen came in the night, carrying away naughty children in their long, black arms. It was said that their flesh was so dark that at night you could only see their empty white eyes, and if you made eye contact, they'd rush over and suck out your soul.

The thought of killing one enderman, let alone several, was not something that Dave was keen on. But if it was the only way, then he had no choice: he'd promised himself he'd slay the ender dragon before Steve, and he intended to keep that promise. Anyway, he had a diamond sword now. If he could get some diamond armor as well, nothing would be able to stop him. At least that was what he hoped.

Blaze powder seemed even more complicated to acquire. According to the book, it was made from blaze rods, which were dropped by creatures called blazes when slain. Dave had never heard of blazes, but he'd heard of the place they came from: *The Nether*.

There were plenty of legends about the Nether as well. According to the stories Dave had heard, it was a vast, hellish landscape of endless lava, populated by gigantic gray floating creatures called ghasts. If they spotted you, they'd blast you with fire.

The book gave detailed instructions of how to get to the Nether as well. To create a portal to get there you needed a block called obsidian, which was found deep underground.

As Dave went to sleep that night, he thought about all

the work they were going to have to do to get ender eyes, and cursed Steve for stealing the ones he'd originally had. He wondered where Steve was now. With the head start he'd had, he might have already reached the End and killed the dragon.

The next morning Dave made breakfast for the others, then told them his plan.

"First of all, we need to do some mining," he said. "We need diamonds for armor and tools, and obsidian for building a nether portal."

"A nether portal?" said Porkins, looking shocked. "You want to go to the Nether?"

"I don't want to go, I have to go," said Dave. "I need blaze rods."

"I—I can't go with you, old chap," Porkins said. "I can't go to the Nether." For once he didn't look cheery—in fact, he looked sad.

"What's the matter?" said Carl, mockingly. "Scared of ghasts?"

"I come from the Nether," Porkins said. "Until a short while ago, I lived there. But then something horrible happened."

Porkins looked as if he was going to cry.

"You don't have to tell us what happened if you don't want to," Dave said, putting a hand on his shoulder.

"No, tell us," said Carl. "I love horror stories."

"My people, the pigmen, have lived in the Nether for generations," Porkins said. "It's a hard place, but we had a good life there. Until one year ago, a strange man came to visit us. Do you know the hero Steve?"

"All too well," said Dave.

"Well this man looked just like him," said Porkins. "Apart from his eyes were white. He called himself Herobrine."

As Porkins said the word *Herobrine* a shiver went down Dave's spine, and at the same moment the wind pushed open the door to their cabin, whistling eerily. He went over and closed it. He'd never heard that name before, but something about it chilled him to the bone.

"My people were always being attacked by ghasts," Porkins went on, "and the man promised he could make us stronger, so we'd be able to fight back. Our leaders agreed, and Herobrine gave us all a potion to drink.

"I was the only one who didn't trust this chap Herobrine, so I never drank mine. But everyone else did. By morning, Herobrine had gone, and my people had been transformed into mindless, bloodthirsty zombies.

"Even my own parents didn't recognize me, and tried to attack me. I ran as fast as I could, until I found a nether portal inside an old fortress and used it to come to your world. I've been here ever since."

Porkins's eyes were red and wet by the time he finished his story. Dave handed him a block of wool to wipe his face with.

"Thank you," said Porkins. "I hope you understand why I can't go with you. I can't stand to see my people like that—reduced to being mindless zombies."

"I understand," said Dave. "Carl and I will go by ourselves."

"Hey," said Carl, "I don't remember volunteering for that! I'm not going to the Nether."

"What's the matter," Dave asked with a smile, "afraid of ghasts?"

Carl frowned.

"Very funny," he said.

Over the next few days, they set to work mining for diamond and obsidian. Each morning they noticed that a few blocks had been moved around in the night, which Carl said was a clear sign that there were endermen about. Dave didn't fancy facing endermen without a full suit of armor though, so at night they all stayed inside the cabin.

One night it rained, and they heard screaming outside.

"It sounds like someone's in trouble," said Dave, grabbing his sword. "We've got to help them!"

"No," said Carl, "those are endermen. Water kills them, so when it rains they keep teleporting to find somewhere dry to hide."

"I hope they don't teleport in here," said Dave, nervously.

Within a week, they'd managed to get enough diamond so that they all had diamond swords and pickaxes. After a couple more days they had enough obsidian to build a portal.

Dave placed the obsidian blocks in place, creating the portal.

"Now we just need to light it," he told the others. "It's late now, let's wait until tomorrow."

Even unlit, Dave could sense something dark and mysterious coming from the portal. The sun was shining brightly, but the obsidian was as dark as night. He wasn't looking forward to going through it, but he had no choice.

In the morning, Dave used some flint and steel to light the portal, following the instructions in his book. Instantly a rippling purple forcefield appeared inside it. When he cautiously stepped closer he could hear strange noises coming from within.

"Well," he said to Porkins, "I guess this is it. We'll see you when we get back."

Porkins sighed.

"I'm coming with you," he said. "You and Carl are all the family I've got, old chap. I'm going to help you."

Dave gave Porkins a hug. It seemed like the right thing

to do.

"Well," said Dave, "I'm glad to have you with me."

"Can we stop all this lovey-dovey stuff and get on with this?" Carl said. "The quicker we get in the Nether, the quicker we can leave!"

So they all stood in front of the portal, their weapons at the ready for whatever they might find in there.

They were an unlikely trio, Dave thought to himself, a villager, a pigman and a creeper, but Dave felt safer knowing he was with friends.

"Ok," said Dave, "here goes nothing."

He stepped into the portal...

CHAPTER SEVEN
The Nether

"Run, chaps!" Porkins yelled.

Dave barely had time to get his bearings before Porkins grabbed him by the hand and started running.

Dave looked round and saw the biggest mob he'd even seen: a huge, floating white block with tentacles, its red eyes fixed on Dave and his friends.

A ghast, Dave knew. From the tales he'd heard about them he knew they were not to be messed with.

With a flick of its tentacles the ghast flung a firebolt at them. It landed just short, the huge explosion hurting Dave's eardrums.

Where's Carl? Dave wondered suddenly, but then he saw that Porkins was carrying him. The creeper was so small that Porkins was holding him with one arm.

"Lovely home you have here," Carl yelled at the pigman. "Oh yes, the Nether is a great place!"

Porkins ignored him.

"Through here," Porkins said, running down a small passage in the rock. "It won't be able to follow us."

Dave followed Porkins through the small hole. He looked round and saw the ghast behind them, too big to fit in the passageway. It screamed in frustration and started hurling firebolts at the rock.

"We'd better get a move on or it'll blast its way through to us," Dave said. He and Porkins followed the narrow passageway until they were sure they'd lost the ghast. They kept going and eventually came to another opening. Dave walked out and got his first proper look at the Nether.

An endless cavern stretched out before him. The sky was nowhere to be seen, but somehow the cavern was perfectly lit. Even when they'd gone through the narrow passageway, Dave recalled, it hadn't been too dark.

The cavern was made of a reddish block Dave was unfamiliar with, but every so often there were patches of other blocks, including some glowing blocks that hung in clusters from the ceiling. The most striking thing, however, was the sea of lava that stretched out in every direction. He could see fires raging in the distance: the reddish blocks themselves seemed to be burning.

It was a truly dismal place, but Dave knew that it was Porkins's home so he kept his negative thoughts to himself.

Carl, however, wasn't so kind.

"This place is a dump," Carl said. "I mean, I used to live in a cave, but at least it wasn't full of lava."

Dave heard a strange noise in the distance.

"What is that?" he asked Porkins. "It sounds like... it sounds like crying."

"Ghasts," said Porkins solemnly, pointing at some white blobs in the distance. Dave hadn't noticed them before.

Unlike the one who'd attacked them when they came out of the portal, these ghasts had closed eyes. They looked almost like they were crying.

"They stay like that until they attack," Porkins told them. "My friends and I used to listen out for their crying to make sure they never took us unawares. Before Herobrine..."

Dave had never seen Porkins like this. Normally the pigman was jolly and chipper, always smiling. But coming back to the Nether seemed to have drained all the happiness out of him.

The pigmen had lived here once, Porkins had told Dave and Carl. Then a man named Herobrine had tricked them into becoming mindless zombies. As far as Porkins knew, he was the last normal pigman left.

Dave had a look round the cavern, but he couldn't see any zombie pigmen, thankfully.

"Come on then," Carl said, "what are we looking for? Let's get what we need and leave here as soon as we can."

Porkins sighed sadly.

"We'll need to find a fortress," the pigman told them. "That's where the blazes are."

"Were the fortresses where your people lived?" Dave asked. "Before... you know."

"No," said Porkins, "me and my chaps were a nomadic people."

"What's that mean?" Carl asked. "Were you gnomes?"

"Nomadic," Dave said, "not gnome-madic. I think it means they moved from place to place, with no fixed home. Is that right?"

"Yes," said Porkins with a smile, "we roamed across the land, collecting mushrooms and avoiding ghasts. It was a good life."

Porkins looked wistfully across the lava, the smile still on his face. The memory of the old days seemed to have brought a bit of the old Porkins back: the jolly pigman who Dave had first met.

Suddenly they heard a sound nearby. To Dave it sounded like a pig squealing, but there was something off about it. It was deeper than the sound a pig normally made, and a bit more... *rotten*.

Dave looked to his left and saw a huge crowd of zombies gathered together on a rocky plain below them.

No... at first they looked like zombies, but they were different somehow. A lot of their flesh had melted off to reveal the bone or turned green, but Dave could tell they had once looked just like Porkins.

Zombie pigmen.

"Does anyone else not see all the zombies?" Carl whispered. "We need to get out of here!"

"No," said Porkins sadly. "They won't harm us. They're my people."

And he walked towards the crowd of zombie pigmen.

CHAPTER EIGHT
The Pigmen

At first Dave thought Porkins was crazy, but then he realized he was right: the zombie pigmen kept themselves to themselves as Porkins walked slowly through them. They seemed slightly less mindless than normal zombies, but they still seemed to have little clue what was going on. As Porkins walked through them they just looked at him with mild curiosity and made grunting sounds.

Dave found it hard to imagine that these creatures had once been like Porkins, intelligent pigmen who could speak. The noises they made now sounded more like pigs, with the occasional zombie sound thrown in as well.

"Come on," Dave said to Carl, "let's follow him."

"You two idiots are gonna get me killed one day, I just know it!" Carl sighed.

"You're a creeper!" Dave said. "I thought your dearest wish was to blow yourself up?"

"Yes," said Carl. "Blow myself up. Not get eaten by

zombie pigmen or get destroyed by a ghast."

"Fair enough," said Dave.

Dave and Carl walked nervously through the horde of zombie pigmen. A couple of the pigmen gave them curious looks, but most didn't even notice them.

"Meet my people," Porkins said sadly. "I'm not sure if I knew these chaps—hard to tell with their flesh all rotted off. But they were my people, nonetheless."

"I'm sorry," Dave said.

What else was there to say?

"Let's keep going and find a fortress," Porkins said. "There are quite a few throughout the Nether, ruins of an ancient civilization. Some of my people used to say that the blazes are all that's left of the Old People who built the fortresses. Either the Old People transformed into blazes or the Old People created the blazes and the blazes wiped them out. The stories differ, depending who you ask. Either way, the blazes are the only things that live in the fortresses now. Well, there are rumors of other creatures living in the depths, but I've never seen them."

"How hard will they be to slay?" Dave asked. "The blazes I mean."

"I've never slain one myself," Porkins said, "but from what I hear, it shouldn't be too hard. Especially with our diamond swords."

The three of them walked on through the Nether,

making sure to keep out of sight of the ghasts that floated above. There was something depressing about the Nether, Dave thought. It was the fact that it was all so similar—wherever he looked there were lava seas and red blocks, there was no variety. No different biomes.

There were no days or nights either, and Dave found it impossible to keep track of time. Eventually he, Porkins and Carl all began to feel sleepy, so they dug themselves a small cave in the rock, so they could sleep without being disturbed by ghasts.

Dave wished he had brought a bed with him; the three of them had no choice but to sleep on the hard floor. It took Dave a long time to get to sleep, but somehow he managed it. He dreamed of the green hills of his home—the home Steve had so callously destroyed—and of his dad's cooking. He hoped that wherever they were, his parents and his fellow villagers were ok.

In his dream he was just about to tuck into a nice porkchop when he was suddenly woken by someone picking him up.

"What are you doing?" he yelled, waking up to find himself surrounded by zombie pigman. One of them had picked him up and thrown him over its shoulder. Other zombie pigman had grabbed Carl and Porkins as well.

"Let us go, you fiends!" Porkins yelled. "Unhand us this instant!"

"Yeah, let us go you freaks!" Carl said.

In response the pigmen just snorted, and carried them out of the cave.

CHAPTER NINE

Caught

Even if he could have struggled free, Dave and his friends were surrounded by hundreds of zombie pigmen, all marching in the same direction.

"Where are they taking us?" Dave asked Porkins, who was being carried by the zombie pigman next to him.

"I've no clue, old bean," Porkins said. "Maybe to cook and eat us?"

"Thanks Porkins," Carl said, rolling his eyes. "Very reassuring."

As far as Dave could see, the pigmen had left his and Porkins's bags and all their weapons behind in the cave. He tried to keep track of the route they were taking, so he could go back for the bags when (or *if*) they escaped, but everything in the Nether was so similar that he soon lost his bearings.

They came round a corner and suddenly Dave forgot about the bags. In fact, he forgot about everything. Up ahead was the biggest building Dave had ever seen. Colossal pillars rose out of the lava, holding up wide bridges that seemed to go nowhere. Dave supposed the bridges must have led somewhere at one point, but that must have been a long time ago. The bridges led away from a huge building built into the rock.

At first Dave thought the fortress was black, but then he realized it was a very dark purple. It seemed to eat the light. It was a dark and foreboding place and Dave had no desire to enter it, but it seemed like he had little choice—that seemed to be where the pigmen were bringing them.

A nether fortress, Dave thought. Whatever he'd been expecting a nether fortress to look like, this wasn't it.

"Seriously chaps," Porkins said to the zombies, "put us down and we'll say no more about this. I used to be one of you, you know. Or rather, you used to be one of me."

The zombie pigmen ignored him.

They were almost at the fortress. Dave could see where the pigmen were bringing them now: a small doorway in the rock that surely led up to the fortress. If they were going to get out of this they had to act fast. But what could they do?

Then Dave saw a ghast floating high above them, and he came up with a plan.

"Hey you!" he yelled up at the ghast. A few of the pigmen looked round at him, snorting in confusion.

The ghast didn't look as if it had heard him, so he shouted again:

"HEY YOU!"

This time it heard him. In a second its sad, crying face transformed, its eyes glowing red with anger.

The ghast shrieked, swooping down towards them. The pigmen started running about in terror. As dumb as they were, they knew to run from a ghast.

The pigman carrying Dave dropped him, then fled for its life, snorting wildly. Dave looked round and saw Porkins and Carl had also been dropped.

"Run!" Dave shouted at them.

"Always with the running," Carl sighed. "Before I met you two I only ever walked. I miss walking."

The three of them dodged out of the way just in time to avoid being blown up by a fireball from the ghast. They ran away from the fortress, running down a narrow passageway in the rock.

"I think we're safe," Dave said. He stuck his head out of the entrance.

The ghast was firing fireballs at the fleeing pigmen, who were running off in every direction, squealing and screaming.

"What now, old bean?" Porkins whispered. "There's the fortress, but it looks like the zombie chaps live there now."

"If only we had our weapons," Dave sighed. "I tried to keep track of the route the zombie pigmen took us, but it was no use. We'll never find our way back to that cave."

"Don't be so sure," Porkins grinned. He poked his squishy pig nose. "A pigman's sense of smell is second to none—and I can smell the baked potato you left in your bag, even from here!"

"Hey," said Carl. "That's *my* baked potato, not Dave's."

"It doesn't matter whose baked potato it is," Dave said. "That's great, Porkins! Please, lead us back to the bags!"

Porkins trotted off happily, Dave following behind.

"My baked potato," Carl muttered to himself.

CHAPTER TEN

Entering the Fortress

Porkins's nose was as good as he promised: soon he, Dave and Carl were back at the cave where the zombies had captured them.

They checked their bags and saw that, thankfully, nothing had been touched.

"Come to Daddy!" Carl said, taking a big bite out of his baked potato. In a couple of bites he'd devoured the whole thing.

"Ah lub baked botatohs," he told them, his mouth stuffed full of potato.

"I can see that," said Dave. "Although isn't it a bit cold?"

"So what now?" Porkins asked. "Do we storm the fortress, swords in hand?"

"I guess," Dave said. "But Porkins, If we did that we'd probably have to slay some zombie pigmen. I can't ask you to do that."

Porkins sighed sadly.

"Yes you can," he said. "Those *things* aren't my people anymore, they're just mindless zombies. My people are gone."

"Either way," Carl said, "we can't just march in there and cut through hordes of zombies. Even with our diamond swords we'll be outmatched."

"Another thing I've been wondering," Dave added, "is will there be any blazes left? If the pigmen have taken over that fortress, surely they would have slain them all."

Porkins thought for a moment.

"Maybe we should keep going then chaps, find another fortress."

The others agreed that this was probably a good idea. According to Porkins, the zombie pigmen didn't usually stay in fortresses. There was no point in trying to sneak into this fortress when they might find an empty one somewhere else.

Before they left the cave, Dave checked his backpack.

Good, he thought to himself, *it's still there.*

Before they entered the nether portal, Dave had packed some spare obsidian in his bag, in case they couldn't find their way back to their original portal. According to his crafting book, you could build portals in the Nether as well. Where it would bring them was anyone's guess, as the book said time and space flowed a bit differently in the Nether, but at least they would be able to get back.

They left the cave and made their way around the lava sea, making sure to keep to the shadows. The last thing they wanted was to be spotted by more pigmen—or a ghast.

As they came close to the fortress—the one the pigmen had taken over—they could see zombie pigmen marching along the walkways and at the small windows. Dave and his friends kept low and out of sight, and finally came to another small passageway through the rock.

"What does your nose tell you about this route?" Dave asked Porkins. Porkins stepped forward and took a sniff.

"I can't smell anything funny," he said. "No pigmen or ghasts, anyway."

"That's good enough for me," said Dave.

Dave led the way, his diamond sword at the ready. Even in an underground tunnel like this, it never got dark in the Nether, so they had no need for torches.

They walked and walked, following the twists and turns of the underground passage, until finally they found themselves coming up to a corridor made of purple brick.

"Nether brick," Porkins whispered. "Crumbs, we must have ended up underneath the fortress. Let's go back the other way."

Dave was about to agree with him, when suddenly he

heard a sound up ahead: a deep, almost robotic groan.

"What's that?" he wondered aloud. It didn't sound like a ghast or a pigman.

"If I'm not mistaken," said Porkins excitedly, "I think that's the chap we've been looking for—I think that's a blaze!"

CHAPTER ELEVEN

Blazes

They crept slowly down the purple corridor. There were no windows, and Dave guessed they must be deep underneath the fortress.

"There's no sign of any pigmen," he whispered.

"Oh I'm sure they'll turn up," said Carl. "They'll turn up, you'll yell *run!* and we'll all have to run for our lives again. That's the way these things normally pan out."

They came to a place where the corridor split off in different directions. Porkins sniffed the air.

"This way," he said.

They followed him down the corridor.

"Wait a minute," Dave said to the others. He stopped to look at a carving on the wall.

The carving looked very old, and it had worn away or been broken in a few places. The Nether brick itself had been carved. Dave assumed it must have been made by the people who built the fortress, however many years ago that was.

In the carving were creatures with long arms and legs. They looked a bit like the pictures of endermen Dave had seen in his book, although in the carving they were wearing clothes. As far as Dave knew, endermen never wore clothes.

The creatures were all kneeling down, as if they were praying, and in the middle of them stood a man.

Steve, Dave thought. *That's Steve! How old is he?*

But no, it couldn't have been Steve. There was something about the figure—its blank eyes—that creeped Dave out.

"That's the scoundrel who tricked my people!" Porkins said, looking at the carving. "That's Herobrine!"

Herobrine. The last time Porkins had said that name, Dave had felt a strange sense of fear he couldn't explain, and this time was no different. He leaned forward, getting a closer look at the carving, when suddenly there was a noise from down the corridor: another strange groaning sound. A blaze.

The sound was louder this time—they were getting closer. There seemed to be several creatures groaning back and forth, and making strange metallic sounds.

"I think there's a few of them," said Porkins.

"Woop-di-do," said Carl miserably.

Up ahead was a small open doorway on the side of the

corridor. They all looked through, being careful to keep quiet.

Through the doorway the floor dropped down, and they found themselves looking down on a small room. It had what looked like a cage in the middle, with three of the strangest creatures Dave had ever seen floating around it, dancing around the cage in circles.

Each blaze had a yellow head, floating on top of a body of smoke. Strange yellow poles floated in the smoke too, though if they were limbs or weapons or what, Dave didn't know.

They had eyes, but no mouths or noses. Dave thought their heads looked a bit like Steve's, and he found himself thinking about what Porkins had told them about blazes:

Either the Old People transformed into blazes or the Old People created the blazes and the blazes wiped them out. The stories differ, depending who you ask.

Could the blazes have been some old race that had become monsters? It seemed possible to Dave, but now was no time to be thinking about history. They had a job to do.

"What's that cage in the middle of the floor?" Dave whispered to Porkins.

"It's a spawn," Porkins whispered back. "That's where blazes come from—or so I've heard. If we kill those blazes, more will come from the spawn."

"That's great!" said Dave.

"Why would that be great?" asked Carl.

"Because," said Dave, that means we can get all the blaze rods we need here."

"Unless we get killed by blazes," said Carl.

"Unless we get killed by blazes," Dave agreed.

CHAPTER TWELVE

Swords at the Ready

According to Porkins, blazes could throw fireballs, so Dave decided they needed a better plan than just to jump down into the room swinging their swords about.

Porkins was the only one with a bow (Dave was annoyed he hadn't thought to build bows for him and Carl before they entered the Nether) so he was going to stay up here and fire arrows at the blazes. Meanwhile Dave was going to jump down and fight the blazes with his sword and shield. Carl was going to cheer them both on.

"Moral support is very important," Carl told them. "My cheering could make all the difference."

Dave hoped that by fighting the blazes both on the ground and with arrows from above they would confuse them, making them easier to defeat.

"We'll keep slaying them as they come out of the spawner until we have plenty of blaze rods," Dave told the other two. They were sitting a short way down the corridor, so the blazes couldn't hear them.

"How are you gonna get out of that room when you're finished?" Carl asked.

"I've got some wood in my bag," Dave said, I'll prepare some stairs.

"Not wooden stairs," Porkins told him, "they might get set alight. You'd be better off using this," he tapped the purple wall, "nether brick stairs."

Dave, Porkins and Carl started digging at the walls, making sure Dave had plenty of nether brick blocks. Then he put a crafting table down (he still had one in his bag) and crafted some stairs.

"Right," said Dave, "I guess we'd better get to it. There's just... there's just one thing. Porkins... how good are you with that bow and arrow?"

"Not too shabby, old chap," Porkins said.

"Good," said Dave. "Just, um, make sure you hit the blazes with your arrows and not me."

They walked back to the doorway.

"Ready?" Dave asked.

The other two nodded. Dave held his sword and shield tightly. His palms felt sweaty, and it wasn't just from the heat.

"ATTACK!" Dave yelled. He jumped down into the small room. The blazes turned in shock to stare at him, then they floated towards him, angry looks on their faces.

Dave held his shield up just in time to block a fireball. At the same time an arrow whizzed over him, hitting one of the blazes right between the eyes. It screamed and span around wildly, and Dave took the opportunity to run forward and slash it with his sword.

The blaze screamed a final time, then exploded in a puff of smoke. All that was left was a glowing yellow rod on the floor.

Dave ran forward and threw the blaze rod over his shoulder into his backpack. He turned just in time to see the other two blazes floating towards him, and another one was forming in the spawner, growing in size.

Two more of Porkins's arrows flew down, hitting each of the blazes in the face. Dave ran forward again and chopped them both into dust. As soon as the other blaze emerged from the spawner, Dave sliced it open with his sword.

Before long Dave had collected loads of blaze rods—so many that his rucksack was almost full.

"Right, that's enough now," Dave yelled, "I'm coming back up!"

He laid down some nether brick stairs and ran up to the doorway.

"What happened to you?" he asked Carl with a grin. "I thought you were meant to be cheering us on?"

Carl shrugged.

"You seemed to be doing alright on your own," the creeper said. "So I thought I'd leave you be."

"I say, we ought to destroy those stairs," Porkins said. "To stop the blazes coming after us."

"Good idea," Dave said. He pulled his pickaxe out, but suddenly they heard a flurry of snorting and footsteps around a bend in the corridor.

"Zombie pigmen!" Dave yelled. "Run!"

"I knew it," Carl sighed. "I knew this was going to end in running!"

They began to run away from the sounds, but then a huge crowd of pigmen ran out from a passage in front of them. They turned round and saw zombie pigmen behind them too. There was no way out.

"We're trapped," Dave said. "Swords at the ready!"

Dave tried to appear brave for Porkins and Carl, but he knew this had to be the end. Even with their diamond swords, they had no chance of defeating this many pigmen.

"Tally ho, chaps," Porkins said sadly. "It's been fun. A real adventure."

"I should have stayed in my cave," said Carl.

But then something strange happened. Instead of charging at them, the pigmen just stood there.

"Why aren't they attacking?" Dave wondered.

Suddenly the zombie pigmen in the corridor in front

of them stepped to the side, putting their backs against the walls to clear some space. Then, the biggest, fattest pigman Dave had ever seen walked between them.

But it wasn't the pigman's huge belly or massive height that caught Dave's eye. It wasn't even the golden crown it wore on its head. It was that fact that it was a *pigman*. Not a zombie pigman, but a regular pigman. Just like Porkins.

Porkins stepped forward, his mouth hanging open in amazement.

"Trotter!" he said. "Is that you?"

"Hello hello, my boy!" the huge pigman said with a smile, his deep voice booming down the corridor. "Yes it's me. And it's *King* Trotter now."

Dave noticed that the huge pigman was holding a golden staff with an emerald on the top. He tapped the staff on the ground and the emerald began to glow.

"Seize them," the big pigman said, the smile disappearing from his face. "Seize them and bring them to my chambers."

"Trotter, what's going on?" Porkins yelled, but suddenly he, Dave and Carl were surrounded by zombie pigmen.

"What's going on is that you're my prisoners, chaps," the big pigman said. "And soon enough, you'll be my slaves."

CHAPTER THIRTEEN
The King of the Pigmen

The three of them were marched down endless nether brick corridors by the zombie pigmen. Every so often they would go up some stairs, and eventually Dave could see the Nether outside the windows. They were no longer underground.

Finally they were marched into a large room. Instead of being made of nether bricks, the walls were made of solid gold blocks, and there was a golden throne in the middle. The big pigman—*Trotter*—was sitting on the throne, waiting for them.

"So good to see you, Porkins," he said. "Welcome to my throne room."

"Who is this fatso?" Carl asked.

"His name is Trotter," Porkins said angrily. "Trotter the Rotter we used to call him—he never was very trustworthy."

"Well, it's King Trotter now," Trotter said, a nasty

smile on his face. "And you'll learn to obey me soon enough."

"How come you didn't turn into a zombie, you scoundrel?" Porkins asked.

"The same reason you didn't, old boy," Trotter said. "Because I didn't drink any of this..."

He tapped his staff on the ground and two zombie pigmen marched over, holding a cauldron of bubbling green liquid.

"The potion Herobrine gave us!" Porkins gasped.

"Yes," Trotter said. "Herobrine came to see me, long before he visited the rest of the pigmen. He told me he was going to trick the pigmen into drinking this potion, so they'd turn into zombies. He offered me this magic staff, saying it could control zombies. With it I could rule all of the Nether!"

"And you accepted his offer," Porkins growled. "You betrayed your people! You really are a rotter, sir. A rotter and a cad!"

"And a king," Trotter grinned. He tapped his staff and the emerald glowed green once more.

"Hold the prisoners still," Trotter told the pigmen. Dave felt two pigmen grab his hands and hold them behind his back. "It's time for them to take their medicine."

Three zombie pigmen walked up to the cauldron with

bottles, scooping up the green liquid.

"They're going to turn us into zombies!" Dave gasped. "Don't drink it!"

But a zombie pigman squeezed his nose and he couldn't help opening his mouth.

"I told you you'd be my slaves," Trotter grinned, leaning back in his throne. "Herobrine gave me this power so that I could build an army in the Nether, ready to fight for him when the time comes. Soon all the realms will be his to rule, and I will command the Nether for him. Praise Herobrine. Praise the Infinite Void."

"Oh my," said Porkins, "we're really in the soup now."

Then they heard sounds coming from down the corridor—the sound of fighting and pigmen squealing.

"Wait a minute, old bean," Porkins said to Dave. "Did you ever destroy those stairs? The ones that led up from the blaze spawn room?"

"Oh," said Dave, suddenly remembering, "I don't think I did."

"What's all that noise?" Trotter growled. There was a hint of nervousness in his voice. He stood up, picking up a huge golden sword. "I say, you out there," he yelled to the zombie pigmen out in the corridor, "what's going on?!"

Suddenly a hoard of blazes burst into the room, spinning wildly. The pigmen were screaming and grunting, doing their best to fight them off.

In the confusion, Dave pulled away from the pigman holding him. He pulled his sword out of his belt and started slashing wildly, attacking the pigmen holding Porkins and Carl.

"Let's get out of here!" he told them.

"You!" Trotter roared. He was ignoring the chaos around him and looking straight at Dave and his friends. "You did this!"

The huge pigman ran towards them, his sword swinging wildly.

"I never thought I'd be the one to say this," said Carl, "but... RUN!"

CHAPTER FOURTEEN

Escape

They ran out of the throne room. The corridors were full of pigmen and blazes fighting—more of each than Dave could count.

They started running down the corridor, trying their best to push through the crowds.

"COME BACK HERE!!"

Trotter burst out of the throne room, sending blazes and pigmen flying.

"YOU CAN'T RUN FROM ME!" he yelled, smashing his way through the crowds of fighting blazes and zombie pigmen towards Dave and his friends.

"We're done for!" Carl moaned.

"Not necessarily," Dave said. He stuck his head out of a window. There was nothing but lava below, so they couldn't jump down, but then he spotted a ghast, floating nearby.

"Hey!" he yelled at the ghast. "Come on! Come and get

us!"

It worked. The ghast's eyes went red and it flicked a fireball at them from its tentacles. Dave, Porkins and Carl dodged out of the way of the window just in time, but Trotter wasn't so lucky. As he ran past the window the fireball came through and hit him.

The huge pigman screamed in pain, and Dave and his friends took the opportunity to run off down the corridor.

"I've got obsidian," Dave told them. "We just have to get somewhere safe and create a portal, then we can get back home."

They suddenly found themselves inside a huge nether brick chamber. The room was full of cauldrons, all full of bubbling green liquid.

"Looks like Herobrine gave Trotter plenty of supplies," Porkins said bitterly.

"Come on," said Dave, "that ghast blast won't have stopped him for long."

He was more right than he knew: at that moment Trotter burst into the room, sword in hand.

"Come on Porkins, old chap," he snarled. "It's your old pal Trotter. I just want to talk."

He charged towards them. Dave braced himself, expecting to be cut in two by Trotter's huge sword, but then Porkins stepped forward.

"You've taken enough from me, already!" Porkins

yelled. "You're not taking my new friends as well!"

He kicked over a cauldron. The green liquid spilled across the floor and Trotter ran right into it. The huge pigman slipped over and fell to the floor, squealing in pain.

"It'll... take more than that... to stop me!" Trotter snarled, getting to his feet. But before he could charge again, Porkins kicked another cauldron over, and another...

As the green liquid stung his feet, Trotter roared, stampeding around like a mad bull, sending cauldron after cauldron falling to the floor. Soon the ground was thick with green liquid, and the huge pigman fell to his knees.

"What... What have you done to me?!" he yelled.

He's turning into a zombie, Dave thought. The green liquid was doing its job: turning the huge pigman's flesh green and exposing the bone underneath.

"My mind..." Trotter squealed. "I can't... I can't think straight..."

"Come on, it's time to go," Dave said.

The others could see he was right. Trotter was confused now, but soon he'd be a mindless zombie—the biggest zombie pigman who ever lived. They didn't want to be around when that happened.

The three of them ran out of the room, leaving Trotter behind.

They ran down endless corridors, deeper and deeper

into the fortress, until finally they came across a room big enough to build a nether portal in.

Dave rummaged in his bag and pulled out his crafting book. He wanted to make sure he got this right—obsidian blocks took a long time to break, so they couldn't afford to make a mistake.

"Four blocks across, five up," he read, trying not to forget, "four across, five up."

He pulled out the obsidian and quickly built the portal. Then a sound came from down the corridor:

"RRROOOAAAR!!!!"

They could hear huge footsteps running towards them.

"I don't want to hassle you Dave, but hurry up!" Carl yelled.

Dave pulled out his flint and steel and lit the portal.

But nothing happened.

He stood back and checked the portal, starting to panic.

"Four across, five high!" he said. "Why's it not working?!"

He tried lighting the portal again, but still nothing happened.

Porkins, who was looking out into the corridor, turned round.

"Come on, old chap!" he said. "Trotter's coming!"

"The portal's not working!" Dave yelled.

Porkins's eyes suddenly went wide.

"That's because those are nether bricks!" he gasped. "You're meant to use obsidian!"

Porkins was right, Dave realized with a start. In his haste to build the portal he'd used the wrong blocks!

"Well come on!" Carl yelled. "Build a new one!"

Dave rummaged in his bag and pulled out a handful of blocks—they were *definitely* obsidian this time.

Four across, five up," he whispered to himself.

He quickly built the portal.

"Done!" he said happily.

"Well light it then, squid for brains!" Carl screamed.

"We've got company!" Porkins yelled.

Porkins ran from the doorway of the room just in time, as suddenly Trotter was there, trying to squeeze through and grab them. He was still wearing his golden crown, but that was the only bit of him that was the same. He was a mindless zombie now, his flesh going green in places and peeling and his eyes dim.

"RRRRAGGGHH!!!!!" zombie Trotter roared at them. There was an endless horde of zombie pigmen behind him, all trying to get through the doorway, but Trotter was so big he was blocking it. He was desperately trying to push through—and he was succeeding.

Dave pulled out his flint and steel once more. This time the portal shimmered into life when he lit it; the purple barrier appearing before them. He'd never seen a more beautiful sight.

"Come on!" Dave yelled.

He grabbed Carl, picked him up and threw him through the portal.

"Hey!" Carl had time to yell, before he disappeared into the purple liquid. Porkins ran forward and jumped through as well. Once his friends were safe, Dave jumped through after them, leaving the Nether behind.

CHAPTER FIFTEEN
Snow

Dave found himself face down in something cold. He sat up and saw he was kneeling in thick snow. After the sticky warmth of the Nether the snow felt refreshing, but he knew he had no time to enjoy it.

He stood up and looked around. All he could see was the portal next to him, the purple light glowing dimly in the dark. It was night time now, and it was snowing fiercely. He could barely see anything.

"Porkins?" he yelled. "Carl?"

"Over here, old chap!"

Porkins was nearby, his head poking out of the snow.

"We need to destroy the portal," Dave yelled, "before —"

Suddenly Trotter burst through the portal, snorting and roaring. He reached a huge zombie hand out to grab Dave, but just missed him. Just like the doorway, the portal was too small for Trotter to get through, but he was pushing with all his might and it wouldn't be long before he made it.

"Destroy it!" Dave yelled to Porkins. The pigman was to the side of the portal, in exactly the right place. Porkins whipped out a diamond pickaxe and starting hacking away at an obsidian block.

Dave waded through the snow, trying to get as far from Trotter's reach as he could.

"Carl?" Dave yelled. "Are you ok?"

The tiny creeper stuck his head out of the snow.

"No thanks to you," he said miserably.

"RRRROOOARRR!!!"

Trotter was almost free now. Porkins was hacking away at the obsidian block for dear life.

Then suddenly it broke. The portal flickered for a moment, and then was gone. Trotter was cut in half at the waist, the half of him that was already through the portal falling into the snow.

"You think he's dead?" Carl asked.

"ROOOAAAARR!!"

Zombie Trotter raised his head, his eyes focusing on Dave. He began pulling himself through the snow with his arms, dragging his severed body along.

"Stop right there, you brute!" Porkins shouted. He raised his bow, but before he could fire Trotter swung his fist at him, sending Porkins flying. Porkins landed in the snow, disappearing from view.

"Porkins!" Dave yelled. Trotter turned back to him, baring his teeth.

Dave picked up Carl and started trudging through the snow as fast as he could, but Trotter was gaining on him. Even without legs the zombie pigman was able to pull himself through the snow faster than Dave was able to wade through it.

Suddenly Dave felt a huge hand grab him. He fell into the snow, dropping Carl. Trotter lifted Dave into the air.

Trotter opened his mouth wide. Dave tried to break free of the zombie pigman's grasp but he was too strong.

He's going to eat me! Dave realized in horror.

Trotter licked his huge lips, his rotten breath stinking up Dave's nostrils.

Then, from nowhere, an arrow appeared between Trotter's eyes. The zombie pigman yelled in pain, dropping Dave into the snow.

Dave looked up as another arrow, then another, then another, struck the zombie pigman. Trotter yelled and flailed his fists around in frustration, trying to find his unseen attacker. Soon Trotter was so full of arrows that he looked like a hedgehog, and with a final "RROOAAR!!" he slumped down in the snow, narrowly avoiding squashing Dave.

There was a *poof* and Trotter was gone. All that was

left of him was a crater in the snow, some rotten flesh and a gold ingot.

Dave got gingerly to his feet. He couldn't see any sign of Porkins or Carl, but he could see something: a rider on horseback coming towards him through the snow.

"Thank you," Dave gasped, realizing the rider must have been the one who fired the arrows.

The rider and his horse were covered from head-to-toe in diamond armor. The rider pulled to a stop in front of Dave, his horse rearing up on its hind legs.

Wow, Dave thought. *Now this is what a *real* hero looks like.*

"Thank you, sir," Dave said. He'd never used the word *sir* before, but it seemed like the right thing to say. "I owe you my life."

The rider removed his diamond helmet.

"No worries, bro," he said. "All in a day's work for a hero!"

"No," Dave said, falling back into the snow. "No, no, no, no, no, no, no! Not you! Anyone but you!"

It was Steve.

EPILOGUE

The man in the blue shirt climbed off of his horse. In front of him lay a huge crater, a few half-destroyed houses around the rim.

This had been a village once, he knew, before it had been destroyed by an explosion.

He knelt down and touched the earth, using the magic the witches had taught him to replay what had happened.

He saw images flashing past his eyes, like reading a storybook: a small, uninteresting village surrounded by hills; another man in a blue shirt building a statue of himself as villagers watched; an explosion.

The man in the blue shirt scowled. He knew who the other blue-shirted man from the vision was: *Steve*. He'd never met Steve, but many people had confused the two of them over the years. He and Steve looked exactly alike, he was told, apart from one feature: their eyes. The man in the blue shirt had completely white eyes.

Herobrine, people called him, although he couldn't recall where the name had come from. He was certainly no hero.

He walked to the edge of the crater. His heart skipped a beat with excitement as he saw what lay below, through a crack in the ground.

A stronghold.

It had been so many years since he'd seen one. He'd thought the Old People had destroyed them all, but two days ago one of his witches had received a vision:

"One of the Old People's fortresses has been uncovered," she'd told him. *"A portal to the End has appeared!"*

Herobrine floated down through the ceiling. The stronghold was in ruins, and the portal was beyond repair, but it gave him hope.

If one stronghold survived, he thought to himself, *there must be more.*

For so long he had thought he would never find his way back to the End, but now there might be a way. If he could find another stronghold, with a working end portal, he could finally complete the mission he'd begun so long ago.

The Old People had perfected travel between all the realms, building fortresses in the Nether, cities in the End and kingdoms under the sea. Herobrine had taught them his magic, and in return they had taught him their own. But when they had learned what he really wanted—his true plan—they had betrayed him.

He had paid them back, of course. There were no Old People left anymore; Herobrine had taken care of that.

He touched the smooth surface of one of the ender portal blocks. Even broken he could feel strong magic coming from it. Using his own power he reached out into the past, to see how it had broken.

A vision came to him: the stronghold closed off from the world, completely in darkness. The portal was complete and working. Suddenly there was a massive explosion from above, caving in the roof and breaking the portal, then Steve and some villagers came down through the roof.

Steve, Herobrine thought angrily, *that fool destroyed the portal.*

The vision continued. The villagers all gathered round the broken portal, speaking words Herobrine couldn't hear. Looking into the past wasn't an exact science, even with his power.

Then one villager, he looked younger than the rest, started speaking. Everyone stopped what they were doing and listened to him. The villager led them all back outside and threw something into the air. Herobrine used all his magic to try and hear what the boy was saying, but he could only make out a few words:

"I'll find the End Portal... slay the ender dragon..."

Herobrine took his hand off the broken ender portal and the vision came to an end.

Could it be true? Could that young villager have discovered a way to find ender portals?

Herobrine closed his eyes. He reached out with his magic, trying to find the information he sought. *The boy's name... what is the boy's name...*

The boy had lived here, this had been his home. The boy was gone, but Herobrine could feel his presence still. People moved from place to place, building their feeble structures, but the ground and the rock remembered.

What is his name? Herobrine asked again. *Tell me his name!*

Finally, the ground whispered back an answer. It was a short answer; a short name.

Herobrine floated back out of the stronghold, landing on the grass on the edge of crater. Two of his witches were waiting for him.

"Well?" one of them asked. "Did you find what you were looking for?"

"Dave," Herobrine whispered. As he spoke the grass for miles around withered and died and the leaves fell from the trees. A nearby herd of cows were suddenly spooked, and ran away as fast as their legs would take them.

"I want you to find someone," he said softly. "A villager. His name... is *Dave*."

TO BE CONTINUED...

Made in the USA
Middletown, DE
05 March 2021